Not Quite a Mermaid

MERMAID FRIENDS

LINDA CHAPMAN

Illustrated by Dawn Apperley

PUFFIN

PUFFIN BOOKS

Published by the Penguin Group
Penguin Books Ltd, 80 Strand, London WC2R 0RL, England
Penguin Group (USA) Inc., 375 Hudson Street, New York,
New York 10014, USA
Penguin Group (Canada), 90 Eglinton Avenue East, Suite 700, Toronto, Ontario,
Canada M4P 2Y3 (a division of Pearson Penguin Canada Inc.)
Penguin Ireland, 25 St Stephen's Green, Dublin 2, Ireland
(a division of Penguin Books Ltd)
Penguin Group (Australia), 250 Camberwell Road, Camberwell,
Victoria 3124, Australia (a division of Pearson Australia Group Pty Ltd)
Penguin Books India Pvt Ltd, 11 Community Centre, Panchsheel Park,
New Delhi – 110 017, India
Penguin Group (NZ), cnr Airborne and Rosedale Roads, Albany,
Auckland 1310, New Zealand (a division of Pearson New Zealand Ltd)
Penguin Books (South Africa) (Pty) Ltd, 24 Sturdee Avenue,
Rosebank, Johannesburg 2196, South Africa

Penguin Books Ltd, Registered Offices: 80 Strand, London WC2R 0RL, England

www.penguin.com

First published 2006
1

Text copyright © Linda Chapman, 2006
Illustrations copyright © Dawn Apperley, 2006
All rights reserved

The moral right of the author and illustrator has been asserted

Set in Palatino by Palimpsest Book Production Limited,
Polmont, Stirlingshire
Made and printed in England by Clays Ltd, St Ives plc

British Library Cataloguing in Publication Data
A CIP catalogue record for this book is available from the British Library

ISBN-13: 978-0-14132-053-3
ISBN-10: 0-141-32053-2

To Lindsey Heaven, my wonderful editor,
for her endless enthusiasm and brilliant ideas.

Contents

Chapter One

Electra the mermaid stuffed a pink bikini into the rucksack she was packing for her school trip. What else did she need? She'd already packed her rolled-up sleeping bag, her mother-of-pearl mirror, a bag of treats for Splash, her pet dolphin, and some sweets for a midnight feast.

Excitement fizzed through her. This school trip was going to be great! She and all her friends were going to Craggy Island for three days. The merchildren weren't usually allowed to go to Craggy Island because it was out in the deep sea where there were all sorts of dangerous creatures like sharks and electric eels. However, once a year, the oldest classes went to stay there with their teachers. Electra thought it sounded brilliant fun. Her mermaid friends were quite happy to stay in the warm safe waters around Mermaid Island where they lived, but Electra was different. She loved having adventures and doing exciting things.

'Electra!' her mum called from the front room of their underwater cave. 'Time to go!'

'Coming, Mum!' Electra shouted

back. Picking up a hairbrush, she made a half-hearted attempt to pull it through  her long red hair but there were so many tangles that the brush kept snagging and catching. Giving up, Electra threw the brush into her rucksack.

'What are you doing, Electra?' Maris, Electra's mum, pulled aside the purple seaweed curtain that hung across the doorway into Electra's bedroom.

'I'm ready now!' Electra said,

wriggling her arms into the rucksack straps and diving past Maris into the front room.

'Oh, no, you're not, young lady!' Maris exclaimed. With a swish of her long silver tail she swam up in front of Electra, her hands on her hips. 'There is no way you're going out with your hair like that.' Reaching over, she picked up her own hairbrush from the coral sideboard. 'Now stand still and let me brush it.'

'Mum,' Electra grumbled, 'I'll be late.' But she knew there was no point in arguing. Her mum, like all the other

mermaids, thought it was important to
have beautifully brushed hair.

At last, Maris was satisfied. 'There,
that looks better.' She dropped a kiss
on Electra's forehead. 'Now, promise
me you'll brush your hair every day
while you're away.'

Electra nodded. 'I promise.' She

glanced at the
cave entrance.
Her friends Sam
and Sasha, the
mer-twins who lived
next door, would be
waiting for her.

'And you'll be
careful, won't you?'
said Maris, her
voice softening
as her green eyes searched Electra's
face. 'You'll do what the teachers say?'

'Of course,' Electra replied, hugging
her mum. 'I always do.'

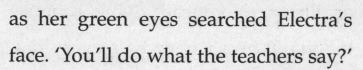

'Hmmm!' Maris raised her eyebrows disbelievingly.

'Can I go now, Mum?' Electra begged.

'All right,' Maris said, giving in. 'Sam and Sasha are going to be wondering where you are.'

They swam to the cave entrance.

Sam and Sasha were waiting outside with Ronan, their dad. Sam was throwing shells for Splash to catch. Sasha was holding Ronan's hand tightly. 'Are you all right, Sasha?' Electra asked, noticing her friend's pale face.

'Sasha's a bit nervous about the trip,' Ronan explained.

'What if I don't like the food, Dad?' Sasha said, her voice wobbly and her eyes welling with tears. 'And what if I miss you?'

Electra felt sorry for her. 'It'll be OK, Sasha,' she said, swimming over.

'You'll be with me and Sam and Splash. Just think of all the fun we're going to have. You and me'll get to share a cave together so we can tell stories at bedtime and,' her voice dropped and she grinned, 'we can have a midnight feast. I've brought some sweets.'

Sasha's eyes widened and she stopped looking quite so scared. 'A midnight feast!'

'It's going to be great fun!' Electra told Sasha. 'Come on, let's go.'

'OK.' Sasha took a deep breath and kissed her dad. 'Bye, Dad!'

'Bye,' Ronan replied. He and Maris

waved them off. 'See you all in a few days!'

With their rucksacks bumping on their backs, Electra, the twins and Splash swam to the gate in the coral reef where they were meeting with the rest of Class Four. Electra had to kick hard to keep up with the twins. She didn't have a tail like they did. It was because she had been born a human.

The merpeople had found her after a dreadful storm. She was just a tiny baby all alone on a life raft. Taking pity on her, they had given her magic sea powder so she could breathe underwater and then they had brought her up as a mermaid. Maris had adopted her and now she couldn't imagine having any other mum.

'Look, there's Solon!' Sam said, pointing towards the coral wall that encircled Mermaid Island. An adult merman was standing by a gate in the wall. A group of merchildren were clustered around him, their tails swishing in the turquoise water. 'We'd better speed up,' Sam urged.

He and Sasha swam on ahead.

Electra kicked hard but she couldn't keep up. Splash came to her rescue.

'Hang on to my fin, Electra,' he whistled. 'I'll pull you.'

She grabbed his fin gratefully. 'Thanks!' she said. Splash wasn't just her pet, he was also her best friend.

They whooshed through the water together and she arrived at Solon's side at the same time as Sam and Sasha.

Solon gave them a pointed look. 'Just in time,' he said, checking their names off the list. 'I hope you've got everything you need.'

Electra thought about the sweets in her rucksack. Oh, yes, she had *everything* she needed!

'Hi,' called Nerissa and Hakim, two of their school friends, as they swam to join the crowd.

'This is scary, isn't it?' Nerissa said, her eyes wide.

'Very!' Hakim put in.

Electra looked out to sea to where the waves were breaking around Craggy Island. She'd swum there once before, when she'd sneaked out on her own. She'd found Splash stranded on a small beach there and she'd rescued him and taken him home. On the way back they had been chased by sharks. It had been very exciting. Electra's blue eyes lit up as she remembered it. Maybe she'd have another adventure this time.

I hope so, she thought.

Solon lifted a conch shell to his lips

and blew it like a horn. Everyone stopped talking and a group of adult merpeople who had been swimming nearby came over. Electra saw that they were armed with spears.

'Now, Class Four. It's time for us to swim to Craggy Island. As you know this means that we have to swim out across the deep sea.'

Sasha let out a little gasp of fear.

'There's nothing to be scared about,'

Solon went on reassuringly. 'We'll have a group of guards to accompany us and there have been no shark sightings for five days now, but I would like you all to swim as quickly as possible.' He opened the gate. 'Is everyone ready?'

The class nodded.

'Then let's go,' Solon said.

'Yippee!' cried Electra and she dived out of the gate into the deep sea.

Chapter Two

As they left the shallow waters around Mermaid Island the sea grew colder. Electra hung on to Splash's fin again so she could keep up with the others. 'Do you remember when I came out to Craggy Island to rescue you?' she asked him. 'You were scared because you thought I was a human.'

'I'd never seen a mermaid with legs before,' Splash told her.

Electra kissed him. 'Are you glad you have now?'

'Very!' said Splash, his dark eyes sparkling.

Solon blew his conch shell. They were near to Craggy Island and the sea was getting choppier. Waves rolled past them, breaking in plumes of white spray as they hit the rocks surrounding the island. One of the rocks was so big it was almost like a mini-island with very pretty green, purple and pink moss growing on the top of it.

That looks like a good place to play, Electra thought to herself.

'We're going to swim round to the other side of the island,' Solon told them all. 'The water's calmer there and I'll be able to show you to the caves we'll be staying in.' He nodded to the mini-island with the moss. 'That big rock is called Sunset Rock – it's out of bounds. That means no one must go on it.'

'Why?' Electra asked.

Solon frowned. 'Because, Electra, the tides come in and out around it, which means that it's easy to get stranded on it. A few years ago, some mermaids on a trip here swam to the top of the rock when the tide was high. They were playing and didn't notice the tide going out. By the time they realized it was too late, the sea was much lower down the rock and they couldn't reach it. It was too far for them to slither down with their tails and they couldn't dive into the water because of the sharp rocks below. They were stuck on the top of Sunset Rock in the hot sun all day.'

The listening merchildren exchanged horrified looks. Merpeople had to keep their tails cool. If they let them dry out the scales burnt and blistered.

'What happened to them?' Sasha asked.

'They had to go home and it took their tails a week to recover,' Solon replied. 'So if I see anyone playing here,' his eyes lingered on Electra for a moment, 'they'll be sent straight home. Do you all understand?'

Electra quickly gave up her idea of climbing on to the rock. She didn't want to be sent home. She nodded along with the others. There'd be other adventures she could have she was sure.

'OK then,' Solon announced. 'Let's

go round the island and find the caves.'

The sea on the far side of the island was much calmer. There was a large sheltered sandy bay in the shape of a crescent moon and a maze of underwater caves. The merchildren in the two older classes from school were already settling in. Some were arranging their sleeping bags in their caves; others were sitting on the beach, their tails flicking into the sparkling rock pools to keep cool as they talked.

Solon showed them to their caves.

Electra, Sasha, Nerissa and Splash were sharing a small cave next door to Sam and Hakim. Each cave was lit by three purple basket sponges filled with green glowing mermaid fire. Electra, Nerissa and Sasha set out their sleeping bags. Electra found a ledge hidden at the back of the cave; it was just perfect for hiding her small stash of sweets.

'Are we going to have the feast tonight?' Nerissa asked, swimming round the cave.

Electra nodded. 'Sam and Hakim can come too. We'll tell them about it at lunchtime.'

'We should decorate the cave!' Sasha said, her eyes shining. 'We could make strings of shells to hang around the roof!'

'Oh, yes,' Nerissa said eagerly. 'That would look really pretty. Come on, let's go to the beach and get started before lunch.'

The three mermaids swam to the

beach and started to collect shells. Splash followed them. He couldn't sit on the beach like they could but he bobbed around in the shallow water while they began to thread cowrie shells on to ribbons of seaweed.

Sitting a little way off from them were two very pretty mermaids from Class Five. They were giggling together and, after a while, they began throwing seaweed at each other.

'Look at Keri and Marina,' Sasha said, watching them.

'Their hair's getting covered in sea-weed!' Nerissa said, wrinkling her nose.

Sasha shuddered. 'I wouldn't like gloopy seaweed like that down my back and over my hair.'

'I think it looks like fun!' Electra said. She glanced down at the pile of shells beside her and sighed. She didn't like doing things that involved sitting still for long. 'I think I might go

and explore the beach,' she said. She knew that Sasha and Nerissa would be quite happy to carry on making the decorations on their own.

'Be careful,' Sasha said anxiously.

'Yes, Mum,' Electra teased.

She jumped to her feet and walked up the beach past Marina and Keri. When she reached the cliff, she began poking around. There were all sorts of interesting things hidden among the boulders and seagrass.

Picking up a piece of polished green glass, an old bottle and a piece of wood worn to a smooth white by the sea, Electra carried them back to the water's edge to show the others. Sasha and Nerissa had gone for a swim in the sea to cool off but Splash was still waiting for her. As she headed towards him, Electra realized Keri and Marina were watching her.

Electra felt a glow of pride. The two older mermaids seemed really good fun. She bet they thought it was cool she could go off exploring. She smiled proudly. Keri whispered something to Marina and the two of them giggled.

Electra hesitated. Why were they

giggling? Keri looked at Electra's legs and whispered to Marina again. This time Electra heard what she was saying. 'Imagine having legs and not a tail! Weird!'

Electra stopped dead. The older mermaids didn't sound like they thought she was cool – they were laughing at her!

Marina noticed her watching. 'Had a nice *walk*?' she said, emphasizing the last word. Keri burst into giggles.

Electra felt confused and hurt. She'd never been teased about having legs before.

'You're not a real mermaid, are you?' Keri said to her. 'You can't be if you've got legs.'

Electra's cheeks burnt with embarrassment. Suddenly she didn't want to be on the beach any longer. Dumping the things she was carrying on to the sand, she dived into the water.

Splash surfaced beside her. 'I heard what those two mermaids said, Electra. Are you all right?' he asked, his dark eyes anxious.

Electra bit her lip. 'I'm fine,' she muttered, but her face still felt hot and there was a hard lump in her throat.

Just then, the others swam over.

'So what did you find?' Sam asked.

'I . . . I found all sorts of bits and pieces,' Electra replied, trying to act as if nothing had happened. 'They're on the beach.'

'Can we see them?' Hakim asked eagerly.

Electra hesitated. She didn't want to go back to the beach while Marina and Keri were there. To her relief, there was the sound of a conch shell blowing.

'That's Solon,' Hakim said, looking round. 'It must be lunchtime, everyone. Come on!'

Chapter Three

After lunch, Class Four spent the rest of the day by the rock pools – lifting stones and fishing out crabs and other sea creatures they found there. It was fun doing something different from normal lessons, and by the end of the day, Electra had almost forgotten about Keri and Marina's comments. But then, as she and her friends were finishing their supper, the two older mermaids came and sat near them.

As Marina and Keri sat down, they looked at Electra and nudged each other. Electra's heart sank. She hoped they weren't going to start teasing her again. 'Are you all ready for the midnight feast tonight?' she said quickly to the others.

They nodded.

'I don't know how we're going to stay awake,' Nerissa said.

'I'll wake you up at midnight if you fall asleep,' Splash offered.

Keri and Marina sidled down the beach towards them. Electra held her breath, but to her relief they didn't say anything about her legs.

'Are you lot planning on having a midnight feast?' Keri asked.

'Yes,' Sasha replied.

'Why?' Electra asked, immediately suspicious.

Keri and Marina exchanged looks.

'Oh, no reason,' Marina said, but a grin flickered around her mouth. She swam up from the table. 'Come on, Keri.'

Keri joined her. Marina whispered something in her ear. Keri laughed and the two of them swam off.

'What was all that about?' Nerissa said, watching them giggling to each other as they left the dining cavern.

Electra swallowed. She didn't want to say anything to her friends but she was sure Marina and Keri had been laughing at her. She stood up. 'Come on,' she said, trying hard not to think about it. 'Let's go back to our caves.'

After arranging to meet at midnight, the girls said goodbye to the boys and swam into their cave with Splash. The baskets of mermaid fire were burning lower now. Nerissa had brought a pack of cards, so they played a noisy game of snap and then Sasha got out a box of small

shells. They took it in turns to brush each other's hair and weave in shell decorations.

'At least I can tell Mum I kept my promise and brushed my hair,' Electra said, yawning. 'Oh, dear, I'm really tired.'

'Me too,' Nerissa agreed. 'I don't know how I'm going to stay awake.'

'Why don't you tell us a story, Electra?' Sasha suggested.

'Yes, tell us one about a sea fairy,' Nerissa put in eagerly. 'I love your stories.'

'OK,' said Electra. 'Let's get into our sleeping bags and I'll think of one.'

They snuggled into their sleeping bags. As Electra got comfortable, Splash came and lay beside her. The mermaid fire was almost out now and shadows flickered over the walls making dark shapes and patterns.

'It's a bit spooky in here,' Sasha commented nervously.

Electra moved closer to Splash. 'It's just shadows,' she said. Taking a deep breath, she began to tell a story. 'Once upon a time, there was an island called Craggy Island. A sea fairy lived there.'

Sasha wriggled happily. 'I think I'm going to like this story.'

'The sea fairy lived right at the very top of the island in a house burrowed into a hill,' Electra continued, her imagination working quickly. 'There was a tiny blue door and a little pebble path that led into her house and inside

the house the
fairy made all
sorts of yummy
sweets.'

'Mmm,' Nerissa sighed.

'One day, the sea fairy, who was called Celestine, was making some sweets when it got all dark and a storm blew up,' Electra went on. 'The trees started creaking and the rain came pouring down, lightning flashed and thunder rumbled.' She wrapped her arms around her legs, pictures flashing through her head. 'It was very scary and then suddenly Celestine heard the

sound of feet coming up her path.
Crunch, crunch, crunch, they went.'

Sasha gave a little gasp. 'Who was it?'

Electra was too caught up in the
story to answer. 'Nearer and nearer
those footsteps came and then all of a
sudden they stopped.'

Sasha grabbed
Nerissa's arm.

'Celestine
went to the
window,'
Electra said. 'She looked
out and she saw . . .'

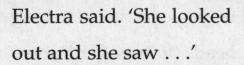

As she paused, a moaning noise

suddenly echoed loudly outside their cave, 'Ooooohhhhhhhh!'

Electra almost jumped out of her skin. Splash swooshed up into the water in alarm.

'Ahhhh!' screamed Sasha and Nerissa.

'Oooooohhhhhhhh!' the horrible sound came again.

'A ghost!' Sasha exclaimed in terror. 'It's a ghost!'

Chapter Four

'Electra!' Splash whistled, sounding frightened.

Nerissa looked pale and Sasha started to cry.

'I want to go home,' Sasha wailed. 'I want my dad!'

'Ooooooohhhhhhhh!'

Electra gasped in alarm but as she did so she heard something that made her frown. It sounded like a giggle.

'Hang on a minute,' she said, suddenly feeling much less scared. She swam to the entrance of the cave.

'Be careful, Electra!' Nerissa called anxiously.

Electra popped her head out of her cave. A white shape was swimming in the water a little way off and muffled chuckling was coming from it.

Looking at the shape more clearly Electra could see that it was an unzipped sleeping bag. Two tails were sticking out of the bottom. It was just a trick!

Diving out of the cave she swam to the shape as the mermaids hiding beneath it began to moan again.

'Oooh– ow!' the moaning broke off in surprise as Electra grabbed the sleeping bag and pulled it off.

Marina and Keri looked out, their eyes gleaming with laughter. 'Tricked you!' Marina laughed.

'You all thought it was a ghost! We heard you scream!' Keri grinned.

As Electra thought of Sasha crying in the cave she felt furious. 'That was a really mean trick to play!'

'But it was funny!' Marina giggled.

Sam and Hakim emerged from their cave. 'What was that noise?' asked Hakim.

'What's going on?' demanded Sam.

Sasha came to the cave entrance with Nerissa. She was still crying. 'I want to go home!'

'It's all right, Sasha,' Electra said, swimming over. 'It was just Keri and Marina playing a trick.'

Nerissa hugged her and Electra turned to glare at the older mermaids.

Keri frowned in concern. 'We didn't mean to really scare you. Are you OK?' she asked, swimming over to Sasha. Sasha cried even harder.

'Just leave her alone!' Electra said angrily.

Keri and Marina swapped worried looks and swam away. They didn't look as if they felt like laughing so much now.

'Come on, Sasha, it's OK,' Electra comforted her. They all went into the girls' cave, the boys too.

'It was just a joke,' said Sam, giving his sister a hug.

'Let's have the midnight feast – then you'll feel better,' Hakim suggested.

Sasha shook her head. 'I don't feel like having a midnight feast now!' she wailed. 'I just want to go to bed.'

Electra thought crossly of the older

mermaids. Now they'd spoilt their midnight feast too. 'That's all right, we can have the feast tomorrow,' she told Sasha. The others nodded and said a rather subdued goodnight to each other. After the boys had gone, the girls got back into their sleeping bags.

'Will you tell me another story, Electra?' Sasha asked. 'A nice one.'

'OK,' Electra agreed. She began to make up a story about the sea fairy making sweets and bringing them to Mermaid Island for a special feast. She kept it as unscary as she could and by the time she was halfway through, Sasha and Nerissa were asleep.

The next morning, when Electra, Sasha and Nerissa went into the dining cavern for breakfast, Keri and Marina were already sitting at the table. Electra's heart sank; she just knew they were going to be mean about her legs again. But when the older mermaids saw Sasha, they looked a bit awkward.

'Are you OK this morning?' Keri asked her.

Sasha nodded and stared at the table.

'Sorry about the ghost thing,' Marina said.

There was an uncomfortable pause.

Marina broke the silence. 'Come on,' she said to Keri. 'Let's go.'

They swam off.

'It was nice of them to say sorry,' Nerissa said.

'It would have been even nicer if

they hadn't played the trick in the first place,' Electra muttered, looking at Sasha's pale face. She sat down. 'Let's eat.'

It was a very hot day and, when morning school was over, Solon said they could have a picnic for lunch. Electra and her friends took their food to the beach and sat by the water's edge. Splash swam in the shallows nearby.

As Sam finished his sandwiches, he looked around. 'Are you going to go exploring today, Electra?'

Electra hesitated. She wanted to but she didn't want to run the risk of being teased by Marina and Keri. She hadn't seen them since breakfast, but she had a feeling that if she went exploring she was bound to bump into them. 'I . . . I don't feel like exploring today,' she said.

The others looked at her in surprise.

'But you *always* feel like exploring,' Splash said from the water.

'Not today,' Electra muttered.

Splash stared at her. 'But . . .'

'It's too hot,' she interrupted him before he could question her further.

'It *is* boiling,' Nerissa said, looking up at the cloudless blue sky. 'Anyone want to come for a swim?'

They all nodded and slipped into the water. As Electra waded in, Splash bobbed up beside her. 'Are you staying here because of Marina and Keri?' he asked.

'Um . . . yes,' Electra reluctantly

admitted. 'I don't want them to tease me again, you know, tell me I'm not a proper mermaid because I haven't got a tail.'

'Well, I'm glad you haven't got a tail,' Splash declared.

Electra looked at him in surprise. 'Why?'

'Because if you had a tail you wouldn't have been able to rescue me that time we first met – when I was stranded on the beach,' replied Splash.

'None of the other mermaids would have been able to run over the rocks like you did.'

'I guess so,' Electra said slowly. She hadn't thought of that.

Splash nudged her. 'You shouldn't let Marina and Keri stop you from exploring if that's what you want to do, Electra. You're really lucky that you *can* go exploring. I think it's great that you've got legs.'

Splash is right, Electra realized. *What does it matter what Keri and Marina say?* Feeling suddenly much happier, she started to swim back towards the beach.

'Where are you going?' Splash called.

'To explore!' she grinned.

Splash clapped his flippers in delight.

Reaching the beach, Electra climbed out of the water. A plan was already forming in her mind. She was going to make the most of her legs and climb all the way to the top of the island!

She ran across the sand and clambered up the cliff. When she reached the top she saw a small hill rising up in the centre of the island. She began to climb it. It was covered with fine grass and flowers. Reaching the very top, Electra stopped and looked all round. There was Mermaid Island in the distance and the dangerous rocks on the other side of Craggy Island.

Something caught her eye. On Sunset Rock she could see two mermaids!

It was Marina and Keri!

Electra gasped. Shading her eyes from the sun, she looked across at them. The rock was sticking far out of the water – the tide must be low. Electra frowned. Keri's face was in her hands and she looked as if she was crying. Peering more closely, Electra saw that Marina seemed to be crying too.

'Oh, no!' Electra cried out as she looked at the jagged sides of Sunset Rock. Marina and Keri were stuck on the top!

Chapter Five

Electra raced down the hill. She didn't know what Marina and Keri were doing on Sunset Rock but she had to get help! She ran towards the cliff but then she stopped. If she went and told Solon he would be really cross with

Marina and Keri and he would send them home. Electra hesitated. Although Marina and Keri had been mean, she didn't want to get them into big trouble with the teachers.

I bet I could help them myself, she thought. *I could swim to the rock, climb up it and help them down into the water.*

Changing direction, she began to run across the cliff top in the direction of Sunset Rock. She scrambled down the cliff face on to the small deserted sandy beach.

'I'm coming!' she shouted.

The older mermaids saw her and

their faces lit up with relief. 'Help us, Electra!' Marina shouted.

Plunging into the sea, Electra started to swim. It was hard avoiding the sharp rocks. The current kept sweeping her against them, but Electra kept her eyes fixed on Sunset Rock. She had to reach it and help Marina and Keri. She kicked hard.

The sides of Sunset Rock loomed up in front of her. Fighting through the waves and half blinded by the spray, she reached out. Her fingers touched the hard side of it and she grasped on.

Marina and Keri were perched on the top of the rock, looking down anxiously at her. They couldn't get to her because they couldn't climb down without legs.

'It's OK,' Electra gasped, beginning to clamber up the rock. 'I'll help you down!'

'Electra!' Keri exclaimed as Electra reached the top. 'I'm so glad to see you.'

'We swam here when the tide was

high,' Marina told her. 'We wanted to pick the sea mosses because we heard you can make them into a shampoo which makes your hair really shiny, but we were so busy picking them that we didn't notice the tide going out. When we did notice, it was too late. We couldn't get down the sides of the rock.'

'It's been so hot, our tails have been

getting really sore,' Keri said, tears filling her eyes.

Electra glanced at their tails. Although the scales looked a bit dry and crinkly they weren't blistered or burnt. 'I can help you down,' she said. 'Once your tails are in the water they'll feel better. Marina, you come first. Wriggle to the edge of the rock and I'll try and carry you down.'

'But I'll be too heavy,' Marina protested. 'I'm bigger than you.'

'It's only a short distance,' Electra said.

Marina wriggled to the edge of the

rock. With a huge effort, Electra picked her up. Marina was heavy, but Electra just about managed to stagger down the rock to the water with Marina in her arms. When Electra felt the water breaking over her feet, she put Marina down. With a sigh of relief, the older mermaid wriggled off the rock and swam thankfully into the sea.

Electra went back for Keri.

'Phew!' Keri gasped as she slid

into the sea and felt the cool water on her tail.

Electra dived into the sea and joined them.

A wave caught her and for a moment she thought she was going to be thrown back against the sharp rocks. But Marina grabbed her. With a powerful swish of her tail, the mermaid pulled Electra out of the swell of the waves.

'Thanks,' Electra said gratefully.

'You're the one who needs thanking,'

Marina said. 'You were brilliant, Electra!'

'How did you know we were here?' Keri asked.

'I decided to climb to the top of the island and when I got up there I saw you,' Electra told her. 'I realized you were stuck and decided I'd better rescue you.'

'It was a really brave thing to do,' Marina said, looking at her with admiration.

'Yeah,' Keri agreed. 'I'm sorry we laughed at you yesterday. Having legs is brilliant. If you'd had a tail you wouldn't have been able to rescue us.'

'We shouldn't have teased you,' Marina said, looking shamefaced. 'It was stupid. I don't know why we did it, but I'm really sorry.'

'It's OK,' Electra said. They did seem genuinely sorry.

Marina swallowed. 'I guess you're going to tell Solon what we did, aren't you?' she said in a small voice.

'Of course not,' Electra said in surprise. 'I wouldn't do that. I don't tell tales.'

'You won't tell, even though we

were on the rock and we shouldn't have been?' Marina said.

'I'm *always* doing things I shouldn't,' Electra replied.

Marina smiled. 'You sound just like us.'

'We should be friends,' Keri declared.

'Yes,' Electra agreed. And she meant it. Now Marina and Keri were being nice to her, Electra found herself really liking them. They were fun and they seemed to like having adventures just as much as she did! 'Just don't pretend to be ghosts at night-time, OK?' she warned them.

'We won't,' said Keri. 'We're really sorry about that too. We didn't mean to frighten Sasha as badly as we did. It was supposed to be just a joke.'

Electra remembered the way she and the others had all jumped and screamed and a grin pulled at her mouth. It had been rather a funny trick

to play. And Marina and Keri really couldn't be blamed for not knowing how nervous Sasha was.

'Did you have your feast afterwards?' Marina asked her.

'No,' Electra answered. 'We'll have it tonight instead.'

'We know a brilliant secret place,' Keri burst out, her eyes lighting up. 'We were going to have a midnight feast there tonight ourselves but, if you like, we could show you where it is and you and your friends could use it instead. It could be our way of saying sorry,' she said.

Marina nodded. 'We can have our feast in our cave.'

'Why don't we all have a feast together, now we're friends?' Electra suggested.

'Yeah!' Marina exclaimed. 'That would be much more fun!'

'Definitely,' Keri agreed.

'That's sorted then.' Electra grinned. 'Let's go and tell the others!'

Chapter Six

Sam, Sasha, Nerissa and Hakim were very surprised when they saw Electra swim back with Marina and Keri.

Electra explained what had been happening.

'Electra saved us,' Keri told everyone.

'And now we're friends,' Electra smiled.

'We're really sorry we scared you all last night,' Marina said to the others. 'We didn't mean to. It was just meant to be a joke.'

'That's OK,' Sasha said, looking a bit embarrassed. 'I guess I was a bit silly. I shouldn't have got quite so scared.'

'We thought we could have a midnight feast together to make up for it,' Keri put in. 'We've got loads of sweets with us – my mum has a sweet shop. We thought we could share them with you.'

Sam grinned. 'Sounds great to me!'

That night, at ten minutes to midnight, Splash woke Electra up. Wriggling out of her sleeping bag, she quickly roused the others. They gathered the sweets together and swam out just as the boys and Marina and Keri came out of their caves. Keri was carrying an enormous bag of sweets.

'It's this way!' she whispered.

They swam silently through the

dark water. All the other caves were quiet. Electra grasped Splash's fin and let him pull her along. Excitement raced through her. Where were they going?

They reached what looked like a blank rocky wall but then Electra saw a crack in it, hidden in the shadows. Marina and Keri slipped inside and the others all followed.

'Oh, wow!' Electra gasped as they swam into a beautiful underwater grotto. The dark blue water was lit up by hundreds of tiny, friendly, pink and turquoise jellyfish. Their bodies glowed and sparkled like tiny stars as they bobbed and floated overhead. There was an empty giant clam shell in the middle of the floor and seven enormous sponges that looked just perfect for sitting on.

Keri swam out of the grotto and reappeared a few moments later with a ball of mermaid fire. She placed it in the clam shell. Green flames flickered and glowed.

'Isn't this the perfect place for a midnight feast?' Keri said to Electra.

'It is,' Electra agreed, looking round in delight. 'It's really magical.'

Sam nudged her. 'Should we share the sweets out now, Electra?'

Sitting on the sponges around the fire, they tipped out all the sweets. With Marina and Keri's as well as Electra's there were loads for everyone – starfish spun from sugar, tiny sea horses made from mermaid sherbet that melted and fizzed on their tongues, shells filled with chocolate cream and long strands of candy seaweed.

'Yum!' Sam said, as he stuffed his mouth full of sherbet sea horses.

'Here, try a strawberry sea slug,' Keri said, offering a box of sweets around.

'I like the chocolate fish,' Marina said, handing round another packet.

Sasha sighed happily and looked up at the dancing jellyfish above. 'This is the best midnight feast ever!'

'Tell us a story, Electra,' Nerissa said.

'I know,' Sasha said. 'Tell us about what it was like standing on top of the island.'

'It was brilliant,' Electra said, her eyes shining at the memory. 'The ground smelt warm and the grass was short and prickly under my feet. There

were little flowers everywhere, pink
and white and purple. They were soft
to walk on and they smelt sweet.
When I was standing on top of the hill,
I could see all around. I saw Mermaid

Island and the
rocks and the
waves breaking
in ripples far
out in the deep
sea.'

'It sounds amazing,' Marina said longingly. 'I wish I could climb up there.'

'Me too,' Keri agreed and the others nodded.

'You *are* lucky, Electra,' Sasha said.

As Electra looked at her friends, old and new, a warm glow spread through her. *Yes,* she thought, *I am.*

Splash nudged her. 'So do you still wish you had a tail, Electra?'

Electra grinned at him happily. 'No.' She put her arm over his back and hugged him. 'I like everything just the way it is!'

Do you love magic, unicorns and fairies?

Join the sparkling

Linda Chapman

fan club today!

It's FREE!

You will receive a sparkle pack, including:

Stickers   **Badge**

Membership card   **Glittery pencil**

Plus four Linda Chapman newsletters every year,
packed full of fun, games, news and competitions.
And look out for a special card on your birthday!

How to join:

Visit lindachapman.co.uk and enter your details

Send your name, address, date of birth* and email address (if you have one) to:

Linda Chapman Fan Club, Puffin Marketing,
80 Strand, London, WC2R 0RL

Your details will be kept by Puffin only for the purpose of sending information regarding Linda Chapman
and other relevant Puffin books. It will not be passed on to any third parties.
You will receive your free introductory pack within 28 days

*If you are under 13, you must get permission from a parent or guardian

Notice to parent/guardian of children under 13 years old: Please add the following to their email/letter including
your name and signature: I consent to my child/ward submitting his/her personal details as above.